WANDERING CAIN

WANDERING CAIN

by

Joe Cohen

REGENT PRESS
Berkeley, California

ISBN 13: 978-1-58790-138-6
ISBN 10: 1-58790-138-2
LCCN: 2007928847

COVER IMAGE: Carved Etowah pebble filled ornament
from *National Graphic Magazine*, Vol. 180, No. 4, Oct 1991, pg. 65,
photographed by Lynn Johnson.

Manufactured in the U.S.A.
REGENT PRESS
Berkeley, California
www.regentpress.net

A man, after he has brushed off the dust and chips of his life, will have only the hard, clean question: Was it good or was it evil? Have I done well—or ill?

JOHN STEINBECK, *EAST OF EDEN*

What have you done?

GENESIS

Prologue

IT COULD HAVE BEEN WORSE; I could have been in Hell, all these millennia, instead of perpetually roaming the Earth.

Nod, my first land of exile, had no sun, only moon, and I lost all sense of time. I don't know whether I dwelt a thousand years or a day, in that gnarly place of shadows, stones, brambles, and strange animals that peered in silence.

At first I raged in anger, wept, cursed God, tried to beguile him with offers of penance, but it was all useless, I was left to despair. My loneliness became so unbearable I wanted death, and I shouted into the void, "Kill me! Kill me!"

The void answered with void.

Roaming was all there was, and I walked relentlessly, though everywhere was the same. When I rested, I would see the faces of my kin, Adam, Eve and Abel, turned away from me, Abel's head crushed and bleeding.

Sometimes the vision enraged me, and I would yell, "It's your fault! Why did you spurn my grain and favor my brother? You made me kill him! I loved my brother! I hate you!"

But it was horrifying, and I would weep and beg for their forgiveness. I balked at asking God's forgiveness because he had made me an enemy.

What did I do? Did I offend him by offering him the best of my crop, that I grew with such care and devotion? Did I offend him by always honoring my mother and father and watching over my little brother?

The strange thing about the void was that it had *presence*, rather than absence, like an eclipse of the heart.

~.~

1

LONG BEFORE my story found its way into the Bible, it was passed on by word of mouth from one generation to another, a cautionary tale of envy, vindictiveness, and disobedience to God.

"Don't be like Cain," parents have admonished warring siblings, "whose anger created a monster sent into darkness."

Perhaps that warning forestalled some brotherly mayhem, and perhaps inadvertently then, some benefit has come out of my transgression. That thought is only marginally comforting, like speculating that because of Hitler's disgrace, few people now slaughter Jews, Gypsies or free thinkers.

In my long existence, I've noticed that bad examples have not prevented more bad examples from springing up to unleash even more harm on the world.

But I'm not the proper one to judge.

I suppose I should be grateful, in some ways. I seem

to have perpetual life, which many would choose, if given a vote. I'm protected from physical damage by this mark on my forehead, a red obloid that resembles the emblem worn by Hindu brahmins. I've walked away from battlefields without a scratch when all around were corpses. I've fought large, tough opponents who couldn't land a blow.

So if I can't die or be physically maimed by others, and I have an ongoing window to history, what is my problem? It is that I hate myself for slaying my brother. It is that God is punishing me.

Nolan, the "man without a country" at least had a defined sentence, after he shouted, "I wish that I may never hear of the United States again!" and was condemned to drift at sea until he died.

The most hardened murderers are given terms of life or death and then allowed to perish. All of history's bloodthirsty conquerors, rulers and torturers have lived their spans and passed on.

Yet my punishment seems set in sidereal time. I can only hope it will end some day, and allow my ashes to merge into the brine.

~.~

2

THE GENESIS STORY relates that "Cain lay with his wife and she became pregnant and gave birth to Enoch." Before that, it says, "Cain went out from the Lord's presence and lived in the land of Nod, east of Eden."

Readers of holy writ may wonder where the wife came from. One day an accursed man is wandering alone in benumbed despair, another day he has a mate.

It wasn't in Nod that I met her, but in a cave in what is now called Slovakia. I was fleeing an angry bear who gave up pursuit when I grabbed vines to pull myself up a steep mountainside. The bear had caught me spearing fish in a stream it didn't want to share.

The woman was making my climb very difficult by throwing rocks. As I got nearer, she screamed and spit on me. I had no choice but to hit her a couple of times and hold her down as she flailed her arms and tried to bite. She did manage to sink her teeth into a shoulder and it hurt like crazy, so I belted her one more time and she lay still.

Crass behavior, yes, but I was unsophisticated then, no more than a caveman.

How did I get from Nod to Middle Europe? I don't know. Time, in my experience, is fluid and incalculable, unlike the predictable regimen calendars display.

It was millennia later, when anthropologists labeled us, that I learned we were "Neanderthals," a bridging from apes to humans, so named because of bones found in Neander, Germany. For the record, we weren't as stupid or brutal as has been depicted. Sure, we had to be tough, it was a hardscrabble life. I'm sure our low-browed contemporaries in Micronesia were privileged to be gentler in nature.

So there we were staring at each other after getting off to a bad start, her expression showing distrust, mine probably the same. Her eyes shifted to the fat trout I'd managed to hang onto during my flight from the bear. I held it up, pointed to her mouth and she nodded avidly in agreement.

There was more trout than either of us needed, but we ate it anyway, her attitude toward me softening as she devoured the salty flesh and grunted in satisfaction. After we picked at our teeth with finbones she dipped a rat pelt in a puddle outside the cave to clean the grease from her face, then redipped it and offered it to me.

Night fell. Glutted and groomed, we went to sleep on opposite sides of the cave. Before the light of dawn I crawled to her side, lay by her and stroked her breasts and behind, hoping she wouldn't struggle. She didn't. Rather, she moaned, and guided my eager member to the moist warmth between her legs. Thus began the first of many couplings that led to the birth of Enoch, our son.

Though we had no more children, there were begettings and begettings through time, spawning a lineage of nomads, musicians and craftsmen, giving the world its store of troubadours, artists, bohemians, beatniks, hippies. Not a bad line, considering my descendants could just as well have evolved into mindless conformists, fanatics, brutal demagogues.

The woman, Aa, as I called her, (she called me the same) was fragile and died of a pleurisy when Enoch was but five years old. I came home from a hunt to find Enoch crying beside her lifeless body. I tried to breathe my own breath into her, but it was useless; she was stiff and cold, her eyes staring into oblivion. Enoch came into my arms and we cried together. I closed her eyes, covered her with a deerskin, carried her body to the river and let the wild torrent whisk it away. The boy and I sat at river's edge until darkness, chanting a dirge of loss and misery.

The world's first city was created out of her vacancy. To mitigate our loneliness, I began a project of piling stones and binding them with river mud. The stones became huts, a storage place, a cistern, an altar. In the center we fashioned an amphitheater, and dug seats around it.

In the beginning, Enoch helped as he could, carrying small rocks, and bits of mud. As the city neared completion, he was fully grown, muscular and energetic, working alongside me stone for stone.

When people from nearby caves at first came to watch, they ridiculed us, twirled fingers around their heads to mime our ostensible craziness, did loopy dances, and laughed. Fid the Strong led his kin on a raid to knock down our walls with tree branches, giving me no choice but to beat him senseless with his own branch, and teach him some manners. After he migrated eastward with his hairy fat mate and cross-eyed daughters, the others decided we were no longer ridiculous, and joined our project. I put them to work building a high wall around the city, to thwart any enemies that might come.

They did come one day, strangers with faces smoother than ours, who stood straighter than us and spoke in a gibberish we couldn't understand. For several days, they watched us from a rise, sometimes pointing and talking animatedly. We feared them.

Hastily, we lay in a store of tubers, roots, acorns, and sealed the gaping wall entrance with mortar and stone. There were some forty of us within the bastion and the strangers numbered about fifteen, all men. They looked to be a hunting party scouting fresh territory.

A problem we had was that while they were shut out, we were sealed in. It was hard to wait, not knowing what the outsiders were going to do. Enoch suggested we dig a tunnel under the outer wall so that a group of us could sneak up on the strangers in the dark and watch them. I thought that made sense, and we did it, creeping up the hill quietly, concealed by the darkness of a clouded moon.

They were gone. A pair of vultures was picking at the carcass of a doe they had left behind. We followed their southward trail for several hours and came upon them, finally, sleeping in a clearing by a stream. Rak the Worrier grabbed a small boulder and mimed smashing a skull and I pulled his ear and told him to set it down.

"There are too many and they would win."

"If we don't kill them, they'll come back with more, and take what we have," Rak opined.

"No," said Enoch. "We'll watch for them every day, and if they come we'll get on the walls and drive them away with stones and spears."

"Maybe they won't come anymore," suggested Ix.

He was the youngest, of us, a bright-eyed fellow who liked to study clouds, gaze at creatures in rain pools and draw pictures on the soil with twigs.

"Here's what I'm going to do," I said. "I'm going to follow them until I know where they come from, and how many there are. You can all go back now, and I'll see you when I see you."

"We won't go back without you," said Enoch.

"Yes, you must." I said. "Go back and protect the city in case others come."

"What if we never see you again?"

The old grief flooded through me. I turned away to collect myself, then looked at my son for the last time. He resembled my brother Abel, with his sure, honest manner. I often wondered how he could trust and love me when the blood of fratricide ran through my veins.

I embraced him, and said, "Go, now."

I watched them disappear into the darkness and resigned myself to walk again in the valley of the shadow of death, shepherded by a strange and remote Lord.

~.~

3

DR. ELOI'S voice came out of the darkness.

"Yes. Continue."

"I don't know if I want to talk any more today."

"Why?"

"It's like talking to an empty room. With your face in the shadows, I don't know if you even exist. Why don't you ever reveal yourself?"

"When it's time to see my face, you will. Tell me more about this feeling of despair."

"What more is there to say? It's clamped around my heart, relentlessly."

"Have you ever contemplated suicide?"

"That's not an option."

"Why not?"

"I can't die until I'm released, and that may never be. I jumped off a cliff once, and as the ground disappeared, I was projected into another epoch. I have no control over my life span."

"Let's talk about this notion that you're an outcast from the Book of Genesis."

"It's not a notion. I'm Cain, son of Adam, son of Eve, brother of Abel."

"All right, then, let's say you're that person. What do you hope to attain by undergoing this psychoanalysis?"

"I want to find out how I'm different from others, why I'm perpetually doomed for my sin, while others seem to get off the hook. I want to know if I have the ability to change or if there's something essentially criminal in me that can't be rooted out."

"Do you feel criminal?"

"Of course."

"Why is that?"

"I've seen, in these many years, the emotional structure of humans leads us to do terrible things. I'm probably no worse than others, but I was first. It seems that when I committed murder, I set the stage for all the mayhem that came after."

"Can you really hold yourself responsible for the violence of this world?"

"In the sense that an ill wind blows no good."

"Let me ask you something. You say you've lived through the ages. Did you know Jesus?"

"Yessua ben Joseph. I didn't really know him, met him a couple of times and heard him preach once, on a hill overlooking Galilee. I was better acquainted with

Magdalen, one of his devotees."

"Tell me about it."

~.~

4

SHE WAS...well, voluptuous and beautiful. I was crazy about her. Like a lot of prostitutes, she only pretended to take pleasure in the sex act, to please her customers. I could sense, when I caressed her, that she wasn't there, that her real self was in another region, but I didn't mind; in fact, it made her all the more interesting, that remoteness.

She had dark hair that cascaded to her shoulders in ringlets, dark eyes, eyebrows always raised in a kind of quizzicalness. Her classic aquiline features looked as though they had been sculpted by a genius. Her skin had a pleasant herbal aroma—perhaps lavender.

When she looked directly into one's eyes, which wasn't often, her gaze seemed to ask, "Do you know who you really are?"

I asked her once what had happened to her, to bring her to such a place in life. She gave me a searching glance, shrugged, and looked away.

"Why do you want to know that?"

"Because I'm smitten with you, because everything about you interests me. If you weren't a whore I'd make you my wife, build you a palace, hire poets to immortalize the soul that shines through you."

She let out an insolent kind of laugh and said, "Real love would do that whether I was a whore or not."

"Yes, it was stupid of me to put it like that. Forgive me. Come with me to the desert, and we'll make a new life. I have some money. We can buy a flock of goats and live as Bedouins, beholden to no one."

"Cain, I know how much jealousy is in you. You would think about all the men I've been with. You would want to kill the first man who looked at me with lust, and many would."

Which was true of course. My fantasy was that after all the men who had touched her, she'd crave only domestic peace and fidelity with me. Yet once she was mine, the mere suspicion of any other man coveting her would probably drive me into a murderous rage. I definitely wasn't good husband material for this charismatic woman.

"You're so strange," she said. "You roam from one place to another as though driven by a demon. It's two months since I last saw you. You tell me you've been to Caesarea. I ask you why and you shrug your shoulders as though it were no matter. Then that haggard, haunted look comes onto your face."

"We're alike in some ways, Magdalen, without hope, in the middle of nowhere."

"That's changed for me, Cain."

"What do you mean?"

"I mean there's someone I met."

Immediately, I felt jealous.

"Who?"

"Yessua ben Joseph, a rabbi from Galilee. He looked into my eyes, and nothing has been the same."

"And he's your lover?"

"No, it's not like that. He loves through the spirit, not the flesh."

I was leery of this. The land was teeming with pseudo prophets, trickster magicians, preachers who claimed to speak with divine authority and ordinary madmen whose brains had been baked by the desert sun. It would have been droll of God to choose such deranged beings as his spokesmen. The previous day, a Jezreelite had been hacked to death after screaming, "You're the scourge of the Earth! Thus speaks God Almighty!" He'd had the poor judgment to shout it at Pilate, the Roman procurator. A genuine visionary could not have been so stupid.

"So, this rabbi, this Yessua, what's he like?"

Magdalen pondered the question for a moment, abstractly fingering her gold necklace.

"He's like an ordinary man, but different. He likes jokes, enjoys his wine and food, and human company. He's broad shouldered and muscular from working as a carpenter, but it was his hands I first noticed when I met him, beautiful strong hands. He clasped my own in his, and it was like a holy vibration went through me. It was like waking from a bad dream and finding I could be free from the traps of my life."

"How did you meet him?"

James of Zebedee called "Son of Thunder" by Yessua brought me to him. Do you know him?"

"Yes."

James had told me how he'd rescued Magdalen from two Roman soldiers after they'd thrown a shroud over her in a Jerusalem alley, attempting to abduct her. He'd heard her screams, ran up, and knocked them unconscious with his staff. She'd probably have been raped by an entire barracks of soldiers, subjected to beatings and possibly death.

"I count him as a friend, a brave and honest man. Sometimes we drink wine and exchange stories, but he never mentioned the teacher Yessua."

"Maybe he thought you weren't ready for salvation."

"And you Magdalen, a cynic who's never believed in anything but the moment, are you ready for it?"

"It's all that matters now."

She was different, graceful in a new way, as though

a fresh breeze was blowing softly through her.

"But you've just been with me."

"Because I like you, not because I'm wicked. Did I ask you for money? Have you seen me whoring in the streets any more?"

"No. I'd like to meet this man who's affected you so much."

"Then come to the olive grove under Mount Moriah at nightfall. He'll be there with his disciples."

It was a bright evening in early October, the evening star glittering below a grinning moon. In the grove, the air was fragrant with an aroma of soil, wildflowers and ripening olives. The rabbi was seated on a bench facing twelve of his disciples, James "thunder" among them. Magdalen sat on the ground adjacent to Yessua.

James sprang up as I approached.

"Cain! How good that you've come!"

He turned to Yessua.

"Master, this is Cain, a wanderer, a teller of tales, a friend."

Yessua smiled and gestured toward the side of the bench opposite Magdalen.

"Sit, brother Cain, and join us. Tell us where you're from and what you do."

"It's as James said. I travel from place to place and tell stories. I tell them in Aramaic, Greek or Latin, according to the listeners. If I'm fortunate, they give me food and lodging and sometimes a few coins."

Yessua studied me for a moment and said, softly, "Yes, you're a wanderer, so you are." Speaking louder, he said, "Honor us, friend, with a tale of a faraway time and place."

"Would you like to hear such a tale?" he asked the disciples.

They rumbled affirmatively.

I began:

"You all know the story in scripture, of Cain and Abel, of how Cain slew his brother in a rage of envy when God favored Abel's offering over his. But you don't know what happened to Cain after God banished him."

"Tell us everything about it!" said the one named Peter.

"It would take many years to tell you everything, but I'll tell you a part of it."

Before I could begin, the redbearded one, Judas, said, "How is it you were named after such a person? And how do you know so much about things of long ago?"

"I've been endowed with a considerable imagination, and as for the origin of my name, only my parents know that, and they are long dead."

"Hush now, and let him tell his story," said Yessua.

I decided to make it very succinct.

"You recall that Cain went out from the Lord's presence and lived in the land of Nod, east of Eden. There, without hope, he suffered a terrible darkness of spirit. After roaming a long time, he decided he could stand it no longer, and lay down on the ashy dust determined to move no more, think no more, feel no more. He would become one with the dust. As he lay there, willing himself into nothing, staring at the moon, the moon's implacable face became sentient and it spoke to him. It said, 'In the realm of death all is nought, but in the realm of life you must change and redeem yourself.'"

"Cain, in his astonishment, bolted upright, and called into the midnight sky: 'How is it you come out of the silence to speak when God says nothing?'"

"There was no answer, and the moon's face continued to smile benignly."

"'Speak again!" Cain shouted. 'Speak to me!'"

"The moon spoke no more but its face was transformed into a sequence of other faces—of animals, humans, ghouls, otherworldly creatures from far reaches of the universe, and finally, the members of Cain's own family, Adam, Eve, and Abel.

"The faces faded and a dazzling shower of rays rained upon him until he reeled and lost all awareness. When he awoke he was gone from Nod to a different land where people wore animal skins and lived in caves. From then on, he roamed the Earth far and wide and witnessed the rise and fall of civilizations, the birth and death of multitudes, and he wondered what was the point of it all."

The assemblage was quiet for a while, pondering the story. Some of the disciples glanced at Yessua to see if his expression offered any guidance. Thomas broke the silence:

"I have often wondered myself, what is the point of being born, having experiences, and then dying. Did Cain find an answer to that?"

"Not that I know of," I said. "Perhaps that's the purpose of his life, to find it."

Addressing Yessua, Thomas asked, "And you, Master? What do you say is the purpose of this life?"

"Let me ask you this," Yessua said to no one in particular. "What does the wise man of Ecclesiastes have to say about the meaning of existence?"

Andrew, an eager glitter in his eyes, leaned forward, and said, "He said it's vain, pointless and repetitive, rabbi. What do you say to that?"

"I think that's true, for many people," said Yessua smiling. "Who can remember what the wise man said in the end? Nobody remembers? What kind of students are you that you remember only the depressing parts of scripture?"

Yessua leaned back and laughed heartily, and the rest of the group, after a moment's surprise, chimed in and laughed with him. When it quieted down, Yessua quoted the final words of Ecclesiastes:

"Now all has been heard;
Here is the conclusion of the matter:
Fear God and keep his commandments,
For this is the whole duty of man.
For God will bring every deed into judgment,
Including every hidden thing,
Whether it is good or evil."

The disciples were thoughtful, after these words, and there was a long pause before anyone spoke. I saw that Magdalen's eyes shone with devotion as she watched her teacher, and I realized, with regret, that we would never embrace again. Before I left, Yessua inquired if I had anything to ask him.

"Only one thing," I said. "Can you give me a mystery to ponder?"

"Think about this, then," said Yessua. "If the kingdom of heaven is within, what is without?"

The next time I saw him, it was Spring, after he had acquired a reputation throughout the land as a healer and a preacher of the "good news." In some quarters, it was said he was the messiah, the one prophesied to bring everlasting peace.

A large crowd had gathered around him on a slope strewn with grasses, small stones and wildflowers, overlooking the Sea of Galilee. The wind that had been blowing robustly as people arrived, settled into a mild breeze before Peter rose and asked the crowd to settle down so Yessua could be heard.

Incidentally, Yessua didn't look like the gentile portraits of him conceived by many European artists. They got the beard and the musculature right, and his hair did come to his shoulders, but his coloring was swarthy rather than fair. Blue eyes were rare in that part of the world, and he certainly didn't have them. His eyes were deep set and dark, his gaze penetrating in a way that could be disarming to someone at odds with himself.

When he began speaking, I had to strain to hear, until the crowd's murmuring subsided. In some of the most eloquent words ever spoken, he enunciated The Beatitudes, later known as the Sermon on the Mount, smiting hypocrisy, elevating generosity, and delving into the relationship of the individual to himself, society and God.

"Blessed are the pure in heart, for they shall know God," was the essence of it. Matthew the Gospel writer later wrote that when he had finished, "The crowds were amazed at his teaching because he taught as one who had authority, and not as their teachers of the law." That was so.

Afterward, he walked among the crowd as his disciples worked to keep people from pressing on him. When he came toward me, I was suddenly overcome with a sense of unworthiness, and turned away so he wouldn't see it on my face. As he passed, he placed his hand on my shoulder and said, "Patience, Cain."

My last sighting of him was in the hallway of the Praetorium dungeons in Jerusalem as Pontius Pilate's soldiers took him off to be crucified. He had been garbed in a purple robe and a crown of thorns, as an imbecilic joke. Leading him away, the soldiers mocked him, calling out, "Hail, king of the Jews!", laughing uproariously and slapping him with the flats of their swords. As we passed I nodded, but his face was downcast with the burden of the cross he was carrying, and I don't know if he recognized me.

I had been arrested on charges of sedition against Rome after a shopkeeper told a centurion he had seen me consorting with some of Yessua's disciples. There was a reward for such denouncings, but knowing how guilt can erode the spirit, I doubt the shopkeeper ever reveled in his boon of silver.

I was thrown into the cell that had been vacated by Yessua. Messages from previous prisoners had been inscribed on the walls, some written in blood, others etched into the stone. One in particular caught my eye, and I wondered who had written it:

I knew her
When the universe exploded into a billion lights,
Magdalen,

Bright dark and brilliant
Whose love and sadness were everywhere.
Desert flowers
Rivers
Dust.
When they took me
And tried me
My agony was in leaving her.
Death was simple.
Lilies grow
In some places
Where we were.

~.~

5

THERE WAS silence from Dr. Eloi, until finally he murmured "hmmm" in his resonant baritone. "Anything else?"

"No."

"That concludes our session, then. You once mentioned the Nazi era. Perhaps we can explore that next time."

~.~

6

CAPTAIN von Aebletz and myself, Captain Cain, were to be presented to the Fuhrer at the War Room in Berlin at 10:30 a.m. January 16, 1943. He would look us over and decide which "Hero of the Eastern Front" would become his personal aide. The other would become personal aide to Joseph Goebbels, Minister of Propaganda.

The truth is, neither of us had performed particularly as heroes, except to endure the bitter cold of Russia for two winters, and the shocking blitz of Stalingrad. We'd been selected because we were tall, well-built, Aryan-looking, and among a very few young field officers to survive the Russian campaign intact of mind and body.

Goebbels had devised the ceremony as one of his publicity stunts to raise the sagging pride and morale of the German people. Photographers and reporters would be on hand to record the event for the greater glory of the Fatherland and we would be driven through the streets in open limousines as crowds of hapless citizens waved their hands in ostensible pride.

"Hurrah von Aebletz! Hurrah Cain!"

Little flags fluttering. Arms springing into the automaton heil. Bogus smiles. Cheers.

Leni Riefenstahl recorded it on her movie camera, facing us, in the lead limousine. Hitler was beside von Aebletz in the next car, and I was seated beside Goebbels (who I despised) in the third.

That's right, Hitler chose von Aebletz. We'd stood in the conference room at rigid attention as he contemplated us closely for a while, looking into our eyes, circling around us, listening to each of us recite a selected line from Nietzsche's maxims: "What does not destroy me makes me stronger."

Von Aebletz had been an actor in civilian life and his recitation was certainly more ringing than mine. Hitler's face lit up with pleasure as he beheld his new protege, and he embraced him and kissed him on both cheeks, like a Frenchman.

I was furious. It was my lot now to be adjutant to the despicable Goebbels, who had a face like a wisecracking ventriloquist's dummy. I would rather have been back with my company in the frozen wastes of Russia than a forced sycophant to this deceitful runt.

"Smile!" he said as we cruised along Wilhelmstrasse.

"You look like you're going to a funeral. Smile and wave and heil."

It was my inclination to tell Goebbels he could cram this farce up his ass, but I worked my smile muscles, which had rarely been used in the last two years, into an upward tilt, and hailed the crowd. I observed that much of the onlookers' enthusiasm was as feigned as my own. Members of the Gestapo were milling about in the crowd exhorting people in the same way Goebbels had exhorted me. I was struck by the appearance of a willowy ash-blonde woman who was staring apathetically at the ground as our limousine approached. She appeared to be age twenty or so, had a sensitive, aesthetic look as though she might be an artist or a poet. I threw one of the bouquets that had landed in our car toward her and she looked up in surprise and caught it. Some people standing near her clapped and cheered. I silently formed the words, "write to me," miming an imaginary pen, and she nodded in comprehension.

"Well done," said Goebbels. "You're getting into the spirit of it."

The procession ended at the Imperial Hotel, which had been converted into luxurious officers' quarters where other "heroes" had been quartered before returning to some dismal combat zone. Fritz Von Aebletz and I were given the royal penthouse, with its commanding view of Berlin, a garden patio, plush furniture, a grand piano.

Fritz epitomized the classic Teutonic look, whereas Goebbles found me somewhat lacking in that regard, and employed a cosmetician to dye my brown hair the color of straw, which made me feel ridiculous, like a bewigged dummy in a window display. Even my goddamned hair was a victim of Goebbels' compulsive prevaricating. Fritz naturally looked as though he could have materialized from one of Wagner's operas, the brave Aryan knight on a quest to rid the Fatherland of dark forces. In spite of myself, I envied him.

I had known him to be a pleasant, ironic fellow during our soldiering in Russia, certainly not an ideologue about Nazism, but his personality had undergone some dramatic changes. A supercilious arrogance had settled in and he became domineering in a way typical of privileged aristocrats I'd observed at Heidelberg. I was first struck by it at breakfast one morning when our manservant, an aging Bavarian, overcooked Fritz' poached eggs. Fritz flung them into the garbage and faced Hans, his hands officiously on his hips.

"If you can't do better than that, old man, we'll send you to a mess hall to cook for enlisted men."

The old butler looked stricken and his face crumpled, as though he might cry.

"Forgive me sir," he said. "I'll be most careful from now on. I assure you."

"See that you are," Fritz said. He grabbed his hat and greatcoat from the rack and headed out the door.

I confronted him in the hallway.

"Why were you so hard on the old man? What's so damned catastrophic about overdone eggs?"

Fritz looked at me impatiently, shrugged, and walked off.

"He should do his job correctly!" he said, as he clacked briskly down the stairway toward a rendezvous with his lord and master.

In another incident, an adolescent cadet from the Hitler Youth brigade was sent to our suite with a written directive from Goebbels that we were to accompany his two nieces to a performance at the Berlin Symphony that night, and be available for press photographs and filming by the great Riefenstahl. Hitler himself, along with his companion Eva Braun, Himmler, Goering, and their ladies, would be sharing the royal box with us.

The messenger did a sharp about-face and turned to go after delivering the orders.

"Stop there, young cadet!" commanded Fritz. "Didn't you ever learn to salute officers?"

"Yes sir, I forgot sir," the youth said, and saluted smartly. As he reached the doorway, Fritz shoved him abruptly from behind.

"See that you don't forget again."

"Jesus Christ, Fritz!" I exclaimed. "What in Hell's

come over you? You're behaving like a martinet. That boy meant no disrespect. And don't look at me with that goddamned sneer on your face. I'm still the senior officer, with six months over you."

"You may be senior now, but we'll see who makes major first."

"Until then, keep your sneers to yourself," I said. "And quit acting like God almighty. You're just an adjutant as a publicity stunt, same as me, nothing more. When they're tired of us, and have enough film, they'll send us back to freeze at the Eastern Front."

"Speak for yourself."

That night Fritz got the stately, beautiful niece who glowed sensuously, and I ended up with the plain one who confided to me during intermission that she was a lesbian, a track star, in love with a ballerina, and had been forced to attend the Beethoven concert by her Uncle Joseph.

"I refused, and he got furious and said if I didn't come he would send me to that breeding hospital where young German women are forced to copulate with selected young soldiers and produce ideal Aryans for the glory of the Third Reich. He's vicious enough to do it, so here I am. I'm sorry you didn't get my sister Frieda. But look at her, with Captain von Aebletz. She's totally smitten. Look at her eyes shine. What does he say that makes her laugh so much?"

"I don't know. He's an actor. He knows how to turn on the charm."

Hitler, too, and his lady Eva, seemed to be swayed by Fritz' charm. They laughed at Fritz' ripostes and gazed at him fondly. I could see that one of us was a potential nephew-in-law of Goebbels, and it wasn't me.

Before intermission ended, I excused myself to get some cigarettes at the bar and I spotted her, the one who'd caught the bouquet at the parade. She was leaning against a pillar, watching as I approached.

"What's your name?" I asked.

"Ilse," she said. "And you, of course, are Captain Cain, war hero, adjutant to the illustrious Goebbels."

"I'm not really a hero. That nonsense was seeded into the newspapers. I was just commander of a rifle company, and I survived."

"So you didn't single-handedly storm a Russian bunker and take forty prisoners?"

"No."

"And you didn't crawl through enemy lines and blow up a supply route?"

"Not in my wildest dreams."

Spontaneously, we broke into laughter.

"And how about the gallant Captain von Aebletz? How much of a hero was he?"

"Less even than I."

Laughter again. I liked the way color spread over

her cheeks when she laughed, and the way her eyes sparkled.

"Are you here with somebody?" I asked.

"No, just myself. I'm a music lover."

"Remember when I saw you at the parade, and gestured for you to write to me?"

"Yes."

"But you didn't write."

"No I was afraid of somebody tracing a letter, but I called the Imperial. The operator told me she couldn't connect private calls that hadn't been authorized by Security. I tried again, and she asked rather sharply for my name and phone number, so I hung up."

"Well, then, give me your number, and I'll call you. I have to report to my hallowed leader tomorrow morning, and I'll be free after that. Perhaps we can meet."

"Perhaps." She wrote the number on a napkin and handed it to me. Before I turned to leave there was a tap on my shoulder. Goebbels.

"The orchestra's returning to the stage, captain. We mustn't let Hilda feel neglected by your absence."

"Of course. I came for cigarettes. Would you like one?"

"No thanks." His hatchet face flashed a look of irritation. "Let's get back to the others."

The noble refrains of Eroica ended; the conductor heiled our box and bowed, and Hitler stood and heiled back. This got a standing ovation from the audience, followed by thundering waves of "Heil!, "Heil!", accompanied by muted rolls from the tympani drums. I scanned the audience for Ilse, but couldn't locate her; I presumed she'd had the sense to slip out before the patriotic commotion began.

A ring of Gestapo held the crowd back as we entered the swastika-flagged limousines in front of the concert hall. More "Heil!" "Heil!" as spotlights danced and Hitler extended his upslanted arm in all directions. I must admit it was intoxicating, this roaring adoration of the crowd. Many of the gleaming, rapt faces around us reflected a kind of religious ecstasy. This was the payoff of power.

With a cordon of black-jacketed SS motorcyclists around us, we roared off to the Imperial Hotel, where Fritz and I were dropped off. Goebbels said a curt "good night" and we shook hands with the nieces and planted polite kisses on their cheeks.

"By the way," said Goebbels to me, "you're free for the next few days. I will be traveling. A messenger will tell you when to report to me again. But Captain von Aebletz, you will report to the Fuhrer in the morning as usual. Heil."

"Heil."

That was the last I ever saw of Joseph Goebbels, Minister of Lies, Fraud and Nonsense.

I called Ilse the next morning and she sounded breathless, frightened.

"Something terrible has happened."

"What do you mean?"

"I can't really talk about it on the telephone, " she said. "Can we meet at the Alexanderplatz, in, say, an hour?"

"I'll be there."

She was seated at the base of a heroic statue, peering through dark glasses, garbed in a long overcoat and wearing a scarf around her head. If she thought that getup disguised her she was mistaken, it only made her look more intriguing.

"Does anybody know you're here?" She looked about nervously. "Does the Gestapo follow you around?"

The only others within view were a teenage couple necking on a bus stop bench and a beggar, hovering under a tree. He was old, hunchbacked, leaning on crutches, definitely not good spy material.

"No, nobody has trailed me. I'm sure of that."

"I don't even know your first name," she said.

"Genesis. But I don't use it. Just call me by my surname, Cain."

"Genesis. What an unusual name."

"My parents were unusual people. You seem agitated, Ilse. What's going on ?"

"I don't know you Cain, but somehow I feel I can

trust you. Let me ask you something. How do you feel about Jews?"

"Jews? I don't really think about them much, one way or the other. I'm not a foam-at-the mouth anti-Semite, if that's what you're asking."

She looked at me carefully for a moment before speaking.

"What if I told you I was Jewish?"

"I would be surprised."

"Well, I am, on my father's side"

"You don't look it. Are you in some kind of trouble?"

"I have to get out of the country as soon as possible or I may get sent to one of those concentration camps. I was stupid about the Nazis; I didn't take them seriously enough.

"My parents and little brother made their way to England two years ago, It had been a secret, supposedly, that my father was Jewish, until he learned from a fellow history professor that his department head had denounced him to the police. I refused to go with them because I wanted to continue my studies at the art institute and thought I would be safe living with my aunt, a Gentile who had been tutor to Kaiser Wilhelm's son.

"But yesterday the police visited my aunt and asked her questions about me, my political views, how I spent my time, who my friends were. My aunt and I agreed that should be my last night at her house. She gave me money to leave the country, and I don't know what to do next. I'm frightened."

It crossed my mind this might be a setup, to test my loyalty, but no, that didn't make any sense; Goebbels wouldn't have brought me all the way from Stalingrad if he didn't think I was squeaky clean. I scrutinized Ilse for a few moments, and my internal lie detector didn't register anything.

"It occurred to me for a moment that you might be faking all this, as a trap," I said, "but I believe you're telling the truth."

She covered her face with her hands and began sobbing.

"Life has become nothing but paranoia and horror."

"Well let's see what we can do about it," I said. "We can't put you on a train to France, it's too risky, even with forged papers. Crossing a frontier border would be even more dangerous, there are patrols. Air travel is out of the question. The best plan would be to get you to the north coast and then to Denmark by boat. From there to England and your family."

"I shouldn't have got you involved, Cain, but I don't know what to do. There's a certain SS colonel—he'd been a dean at the institute—who flirts with me, but I wouldn't dare confide in him. There's something perverse in him."

"Right. So temporarily, you can stay at the suite

with me. Fritz shares it and the story will have to be that you're my girlfriend. That means you'll be in my room. Can you deal with that? "

"Yes."

It turned out to be easier than I hoped, because Fritz brought the shiny-eyed Frieda, niece of Goebbels, home with him that night. They had been making the rounds of night clubs and staggered into the flat boisterously, drunkenly, pausing at the door for a lingering kiss.

"Charmed!" he exclaimed at being introduced to Ilse. He brandished a bottle of champagne he had been carrying and insisted we polish it off. We toasted the fatherland, the fuhrer and the "two most beautiful frauleins in the world," to which they giggled happily. I put a Strauss record on the Victrola and the four of us waltzed elegantly, around and around in circles. It was so pleasant, and Ilse looked so happy, that for the while I forgot the treacherous situation we in.

In the morning, we were awakened by rain pounding on the bedroom window. Ilse murmured softly and turned over to lay her head on my chest.

"Good morning Cain. We did something last night."

"Yes, we did."

"I can feel it still. What if I fall in love with you? How could I leave you then, and go all the way to

England?"

"Because they are looking for you. Because we can reunite after the war."

We merged into it again and again it was exquisite, almost excruciatingly so. Afterwards we lay still, listening to the patter of rain.

"I've never felt like this before," she said.

"Nor I."

"I have a plan," she said. "Let's stay right here in this bed, and make love, and talk, and listen to rain, until we die."

"That's an excellent plan. However, right now, I'm starving, so we'll have to put it off, temporarily. What do you say, we bathe, get dressed, go into the dining room, and have Hans make us some breakfast?"

"Yes! I could eat like a stevedore!"

Hans was jovial, took to Ilse right away, and treated our appetites to eggs benedict, sausages, roasted potatoes, oatmeal, sliced fruit, and coffee sweetened with molasses and thick cream. We wolfed it down as though we hadn't had any food for a week. We dallied over the coffee and gazed at each other smugly, like beggars who had just found a pot of gold. It was impossible for life to get any better than at that moment.

"Cain, I have a secret to tell you."

"Yes?"

"I love you with all my heart."

"That's amazing! That's the same the same secret I was going to tell you!"

We heard Fritz and Frieda murmuring as they approached the dining room. She seated herself, smiling radiantly, as Fritz, standing, rang a water glass with a fork, and said, "I have a most important announcement to make."

We waited expectantly.

"It's raining!"

Frieda chortled and said, "Tell them, you silly fool."

"Yes. The real announcement is that Frieda has consented to be my wife, and we are getting married as soon as we can."

A flurry of cheers, applause and congratulations. It was assured now that Fritz would never have to return to a combat zone.

"And we want you, Cain, to be best man, and you, Ilse, to be a bridesmaid," said Frieda, "if you would so honor us."

Ilse and I exchanged quick glances. Suddenly everything had gotten more bizarre.

"Of course. We'd be delighted," I said.

"We need the blessings of Herr Hitler and Herr Goebbels," Fritz said, but there shouldn't be any problem."

"Not Herr Goebbels anymore, but Uncle Propagada," I said.

This provoked a tentative kind of laughter.

"We'll leave you two betrothed alone now," I said. "I promised to accompany Ilse shopping, and we're off to do that."

It was true we had to go shopping—Ilse, in her haste hadn't packed anything, she had only the clothes on her back and needed enough serviceable clothing and paraphernalia for a journey of uncertain duration. She managed to find it all in one department store, where the manager recognized me, was very unctuous, and refused to take any money.

"For an illustrious hero such as yourself, there is no charge," he said. "Just remember me to the Fuhrer."

"Are you sure? You have to make a living, like everybody else."

"Please, sir, no payment. It is an honor and a privilege to serve you and your lady."

"Well, if you insist. I'll commend you to Hitler."

There were tears in his eyes.

"Oh thank you sir, thank you."

Back at the suite dining room table, Ilse and I discussed the situation.

"We have to move fast, now," I said. "Before the Jew haters trace you to this place. Here's my idea: I can requisition a car and driver from headquarters and have him take us to the northern border tomorrow morning. Once there, I can bribe a fisherman to sail us across to Denmark."

"What do you mean, us ?"

"I'm coming with you. I'm going to defect when we get to England and be done with this stupid war."

"But the English will imprison you."

"Only for the duration of the war. After that, we'll be together always."

Suddenly lse's eyes widened, and she looked frightened. She nodded toward the partially opened door. Fritz was there; he had been listening. He turned and left and there was the sound of the front door slamming.

"Oh Jesus," I said. "We've got to get out of here right now."

On the street, we hastened to the motor pool, where I addressed the sergeant in charge.

"I need a car, sergeant. Immediately."

"Do you have a requisition?"

"No. There isn't time for that. Do you know who I am?"

"Yes sir, the aide to Herr Goebbels."

"Well then, get moving. You know what a temper Goebbels has."

The phone in the office shack began ringing insistently. The sergeant picked it up.

"Yes...Yes."

He watched us with curiosity as he spoke.

"Wait here, I'll get you a car right now," he said, walking away.

Within seconds, a squad of Gestapo appeared from a stairway and surrounded us. There was no escape; running would have been pointless.

"Lieutenant, as your superior officer, I order you to get these men out of our way," I said.

"I can't do that, Captain," he said. "I've been ordered to arrest you."

"Well then, let the young lady go."

"Her too, Captain. Please come with us peacefully."

We were taken to an antechamber of the Gestapo and told to wait. In a minute a colonel entered. He was accompanied by Fritz.

"Is this the Jewess you described, Captain von Aebletz?"

"Yes sir."

"And this is Captain Cain?"

"Yes sir."

"Fritz! What have you done?" I yelled. "How could you do this?"

He glanced at me and looked away quickly, which made me all the more furious. I lunged for the colonel's desk, grabbed an iron statuette, bashed Fritz on the head with it, and he collapsed to the floor in a pool of blood. Before the troops restrained me, I hit him again and he was dead.

~.~

Goebbels fed the press the story that the two heroes of the Eastern Front had been returned to combat at their own request, for the greater glory of Germany.

~.~

Ilse and I were sent to the death camp at Auschwitz.

~.~

6

"YOU COMPLAIN God has continually persecuted you for killing your brother, and yet you tell me stories that have a thread of joy."

As ever, Dr. Eloi was concealed in the shadows and I couldn't see his face. I could only wonder who he really was, what he was like. My occasional attempts to draw him out were invariably met with silence and I indulged in the fantasy he was a madman who had no solid connection with the world beyond the confessional of psychiatry.

"Joy?"

"In every episode, there is a woman you love deeply and who returns your love. What greater joy is there?"

"In every episode, doctor, I lose the woman, and return to unending life loveless and alone."

"We'll leave that for a while. Let me ask you this: In your narratives, you appear and reappear, as a witness to history, whereas others live out their allotted time and pass on. Is there no satisfaction in this deathlessness?"

"Satisfaction? I suppose that would be something like pausing in the ongoing stream and saying 'ah.' No, I've never felt that rhapsodic pause. There's always a dread of what's coming next. History, in my experience, is a series of waves, positive and negative, that roll on without purpose, a panorama of progress and horror, empires built on the slaughter of innocents."

"That's vividly phrased. What does it mean to you?"

"What does it mean? I'll tell you about Auschwitz."

A wave of grief overwhelmed me, and I doubled over with visceral pain and a sharp dizziness. It was a while before I could speak.

~.~

7

FIRST, THERE WAS a little girl, no more than four years old. A soldier, irritated by the child's mother moving too slowly, grabbed the little girl and threw her against the station wall. She didn't utter a sound, just lay bleeding from the head and nose, unconscious, in a heap. When the mother screamed and ran toward her daughter the soldier jabbed her in the throat with his bayonet and she staggered to the child and collapsed on top of her.

Then there was an old man suffering from dementia, who looked bewildered and balked when he was told to climb into the railroad car with the rest of us. The officer in charge hit him on the head with a rifle butt and had some soldiers set him on the traincar roof so that he would be flung off violently as the train sped up. They found this hilarious.

My race had been reclassified as "Jew" by order of Hitler and I was on a train bound for Auschwitz concentration camp along with two thousand others of my new ethnicity. When the train pulled out, there were a hundred bodies arrayed around the station in pools of blood—murdered for being too confused to follow orders correctly, or reluctant to part from a relative, or courageously defiant.

During the long ride, we had to stand, for lack of space, and as the hours passed the smell of feces, urine, vomit, stale breath, perspiration, was overwhelming. Several people keeled over, and we had to pull them to the floor alongside the wall to prevent the rest of us from losing balance and collapsing into a panicked, writhing mass. Twice, the train stopped in the middle of nowhere, and the guards emptied the cars to hose them down and throw out the dead and near-dead.

During the second of those stops I spotted Ilse among a group of prisoners three cars down. She was scanning the crowd, apparently looking for me. She saw me, and waved, calling out, "Cain! Cain!" and ran toward me. The guards yelled for her to stop, and I joined their chorus. "Stop, Ilse, stop! They'll shoot you! Stop! Please!"

In her excitement she ignored it and kept running, a joyful smile on her face.

There was a *kazing!* and she fell to the ground. I sped toward her amid a cacophony of shouts from the guards as shots whizzed around me. I kneeled beside her, raised her. She still had the happy smile on her face but was limp and lifeless, like a rag doll. The bullet had entered her back and shattered her heart. As I held her, the warm blood from her wound soaked into my shirt and onto my chest, her final caress to me.

The old fury arose and I screamed to God, "What have you done, you vile malicious bastard? What harm did she ever do? You're cruel and stupid! I hate you!"

"Don't kill him," I heard an officer say. "He's a special case, ordered here by the fuhrer himself."

I fought like a cornered wolf and managed to bloody six guards before I was subdued, tied with rope, and put in the soldiers' car, where they could keep watch on me. A doctor injected me with something that made my mind reel and I plummeted into darkness praying it was death.

When I awoke a ring of skeletal figures was staring at me silently, their eyes exaggeratedly large in their emaciated faces. I wondered if my blasphemy had landed me in some strange antechamber of Hell, and I lay quietly waiting to see what they were going to do. Finally, one of them addressed me:

"What language do you speak?"

"German," I said, "the same as you."

"Do you know where you are?"

"We were headed for Auschwitz."

"That's where you are. Are you Jewish?"

I could see now they were human, though just barely.

"Yes, Jewish. That's what they tell me."

A siren sounded and the spokesman said, "It's roll call. You've got to go outside for roll call."

"I don't know if I can move."

"They don't actually call us, they count us. If they find you missing they'll come in here, and drag you outside and beat you, perhaps turn the dogs on you or even hang you."

I was lying in a barracks on a bottom shelf of wooden bunks. There were tiers of bunks on three sides of the room and the smell was foul, but not as horrible as the odors in the train car. I struggled to my feet painfully, and followed the others outside, where we lined up in a rectangular formation. A guard sergeant walked by each rectangle and counted the prisoners. After that, the sergeants rattled off, "All present and accounted for" to the camp commandant. Lesser officers were ranged around him, flanked by two soldiers holding vicious-looking attack dogs on leashes. Before dismissal, the commandant, followed by a lieutenant, commenced a close inspection of the ranks.

"He never does this," murmured a man next to me. "I wonder what's up."

The commandant got to our group and stopped in front of me.

"What's your name?" he asked.

"Cain."

"Hmmm." He studied me a moment, and moved on.

When he returned to his facing position, he exhorted us in a pontifical tone:

"Prisoners! You know why you're here. It's because you are enemies of the state, people who can't be integrated into the grand design of national unity. Still, you can find dignity. There is dignity in work. When you go to your assignments today, perform as well as you can and keep in mind that your toil is redemptive. That is all."

A captain stepped forward and announced that before dismissal, there would be a special detail formed to work in a nearby town. He gave out lists to the sergeants and they prodded the designated persons to step forward. They were loaded into a group of trucks parked by the barbed wire fence. "What about our breakfast?" one of them cried out. A guard shoved him roughly onto a truck, and the officer in charge replied, "There will be food for all when we arrive."

Another group of trucks pulled up, filled with prisoners from the womens' side. The trucks slowly rolled toward the main gate, and left the camp.

"That's the last we'll ever see of them!" moaned Reuben, a sallow bony man standing beside me. He was trembling all over, sweating, his voice was raspy.

"What do you mean?"

"I mean they're going off to be murdered. The ovens are shut down for repairs, and they're taking them to be shot and buried in a mass grave. I overheard two sergeants talking about it last night."

"You there! Stop that talking," a guard yelled at us.

"And you stop the murder!" Reuben yelled. "Stop the murder! My brother is on that truck!" The eyes in his yellowed face were wild and unfocused and the sparse hair on his head stood up as though electricity was coursing through him.

"Stop it right now! Stop the murder!" he yelled.

He'd gone quite mad, and began running erratically toward the departing trucks when a guard loosed two dogs and they fell on him with a vengeance, ripping his throat, his face, his arms.

"All right, call them off," said the captain.

When the dogs were back on their leashes, he walked up to Reuben and shot him in the head. Some of the blood splattered onto his elegant overcoat and he removed it, handed it to a corporal and told him to have it cleaned.

"Let that be a lesson to you!" he shouted to the assembled prisoners, and walked off.

It was chilly, overcast, foggy, a dismal kind of weather contrived by nature to express Auschwitz. Those times the sun did shine it was unforgiving like the harsh glare of an interrogation light, illumining the degradation of flesh and spirit.

Before work that morning, an inmate passed out pieces of stale bread and a kind of gruel with bits of lard in it. Another inmate, a "kapo," followed him, calling us "pigs" and "scum," exhorting us to clean our bunk areas and the floor and latrines before we filed out for work. I asked Leopold, the one who'd been explaining things to me, why they allowed the kapo to talk to them like that.

"That's why." He pointed toward the door, where a guard was leaning on the frame, a rifle in his hand.

"If Jacob doesn't play the bully convincingly that guard will shoot him or see that he goes to the gas chamber with the next group. He's buying a few more weeks of life. What would you do yourself, if you were offered that job?"

"I don't know."

Actually I did know; a plan for revolt and vengeance for Ilse sprang into my mind. It would incite brutal retaliation, but every prisoner in the camp was a hostage to doom anyway. It was better to rebel than do nothing.

"Cain! Come with me!"

An SS lieutenant so young he looked barely out of high school stood before me, his hand poised on his pistol holster.

"If I don't come, are you going to shoot me?"

"Yes, you Jewish pig, I'll shoot you." He extracted

the gun from the holster and put it against my temple. I could tell he was bluffing; his manner betrayed an ambivalent nervousness, but I went along with the game. It still felt very odd to be addressed as "Jew."

"Well, if that's the way it is, I have to go with you."

Some of my new roommates stared at me worriedly, as though I were weirdly insane and likely to provoke instant mayhem from our captors. One toothless and hairless fellow was moving his lips rapidly, murmuring some sort of Hebrew prayer, The callow young lieutenant saw an opportunity to strut his authority, and slapped him across the mouth.

"Keep your religious stupidity to yourself," he said. "If your god gave a damn about you, you wouldn't be here."

He had a point there.

"All right let's get going Cain, you miserable stinking Jew."

It would have been a cinch to squeeze this pipsqueak's neck and pop the life out of him but I dismissed the idea. I was curious to learn where we were going and what was next.

The lieutenant and two guards ushered me into the office of the assistant camp commander, a gnomic, slightly cross-eyed little SS colonel named Deutscher, who studied some swastika-stamped documents with feigned interest. After a few moments he dismissed the others, set his pistol on the desk near his hand, and looked up at me.

"You have a chance to survive torture, beatings and death, ex-Captain Cain, if you cooperate with us."

"Cooperate? How?"

"We want you to be our eyes and ears. We've placed you in a barracks that has only German Jews, so language won't be a problem. You are aware by now there are thousands of Poles in this camp, most of them Jews, along with some gentile political enemies, and a number of Gypsies. Before our duty is done, all will be gassed and thrown into the ovens, including the women and children. Here is what I want from you: If you learn of any plots for insurrections or escapes, let us know. If you learn anything about the Polish or Jewish underground, let us know. Give us names and details. Tell us anything the SS and Gestapo might be able to use for intelligence. Somewhere deep down, you are still a German soldier and you can still, in this way, serve the fatherland. What do you say?"

"I'm agreeable to that, colonel," I said, playing along with it.

"Excellent. Lieutenant Gruber, who brought you here, will be your contact. You will be doing ordinary work. Any privileged assignments would arouse suspicion. The story will be that you lied your way into a position as a Bundestag clerk by claiming you had no Jewish forebears and that you were denounced by a former classmate. You can claim assimilation to explain your ignorance of Hebrew and religious matters. That will be all for now. Remember your life depends on how well you cooperate with us."

I was taken to a tiny room in the Administration office where another prisoner, a Polish giant about seven feet tall, with deep pockmarks on his face, tattooed a number on my forearm. Somehow, the pain didn't matter. A rat, sniffing blood, crept out from under a broken floorboard, and moved stealthily toward us. The giant stomped on it and killed it, exclaiming "ahh," in anticipation of a boiled rat feast.

The rest of the day, I was given the relatively easy job of caulking windows in the infirmary to seal out the cold wind. It was a Sunday, and no operations were scheduled. Some twin boys and girls were convalescing from some treatment they had received, their pale faces mottled by dark shadows of angst. One of the girls was weeping quietly, the other children were staring morosely into space. They seemed to be on heavy sedation. I asked the infirmary kapo, a former doctor, what had happened to them.

"You don't want to know," he said.

"I do want to know."

"Doctor Mengele has performed sterilization experiments on their sex organs."

"What!" I shouted.

"Be quiet. You'll have the guards on us."

Some of the children turned toward us listlessly to see what the fuss was about.

"For the love of God," I said, softly. "He's cut up their organs."

"It could be worse," he whispered. "At least they'll live. The Nazis will want to follow the results of the experiments. All the other children will be gassed and put into the ovens."

"And you? What was your role in this?"

"I assisted. I didn't have any choice. They said if I refused, they would torture my wife slowly and horribly before my eyes until she died."

I went into the bathroom to muffle my yells into a towel. I yelled until the vomiting began and my tears mixed with the bile from my stomach.

From the bathroom floor, I stared dully at the ceiling, numb with horror. When my mind cleared, the horror turned to searing anger and I resolved I would do anything I could to defeat this place.

That night, on the hard bunk, with the putrid smell of the barracks, the groaning noises of men around me, the gloom of midnight, my thoughts spun incoherently, a melange of phantasmagoria. Fragments of scenes from thousands of years flickered kaleidoscopically, bereft of meaning, views in a whimsical landscape. Here a valley, there a home, an army, a graveyard, a child's smile, a river of molten lava. a gray sky seen through a bough of leaves, a demonic gloom.

"What?" I was roused by a gentle shaking.

"You were calling out from a nightmare." Leopold, bunked alongside me, had nudged me awake. "You were calling for God." he whispered.

"For God.?"

"Yes. You were saying 'adonai.'"

"Sorry I woke you."

"It's all right. People often call for God in this place. And he doesn't answer."

"And you? Do you call for him too?"

"No. Before I came here I was a rabbi, and to be honest, I wasn't convinced there was a God even then. When we arrived at this pit of Hell my wife was selected for the gas chamber, and I knew that God was nothing more than wishful thinking."

"There is a God, Leopold. I knew him long ago. I've talked with him. Even now, he's present in nothingness."

"What does that mean?"

"It means he's unrevealed, like the darkness of space."

"You've lost me."

"Listen, and try not to judge, until I tell you all of it."

Someone in the tier above coughed, mumbled,

sighed. Another voice said, "Quiet, you two." We moved to the doorway, crouched, and continued our conversation softly, out of hearing range of the others. Every few minutes the door gaps were illumined by the spotlight from the tower, in its arcing search, and I could see the puzzled expression on Leopold's face.

When I finished, he observed me quietly for a while.

"Why have you told me this?"

"Because I trust you. Because it unburdens me to tell it to a rabbi who is dispassionate, and can't be deceived."

"Cain, I don't know what to make of you. You seem like a solid sensible fellow, but your story belies that. I studied psychiatry for a while in Vienna and we never had a case like this, where a patient thought he was a living character from the Torah. Freud might have described it as disassociative sibling rivalry, or some damned thing. You tell it so sincerely I'd like to believe it, but I can't. I think you're delusional and that your perceived connection with the god of the Hebrew bible is an ongoing hallucination. I say this with misgivings and sorrow, because in this place, one is probably better off with a fortifying delusion."

"Leopold, leave at least a little room in your mind for doubt about your doubt," I said.

"Fair enough. I don't have to believe it for it to be true."

The searchlight had stopped moving in its rounds, which meant it was close to dawn, and the arrival of another hellish day.

After "breakfast," Jacob the kapo came through the barracks wielding a rubber truncheon, saying, "Everybody I anoint with this is going to be an artist today. You are going to paint the officer's quarters." He selected five men for the job, including me, whacking us sharply across the back. I shot an angry glance at him, and he struck me again, this time not so hard. One of the guards grabbed the truncheon from him and told him to bend over.

"This is the way to wield discipline," he said, whipping Jacob hard across the buttocks.

"No, no, you're wrong, I know a much better way," said the second guard. He grabbed the truncheon and struck Jacob two more times. "Like this!"

The guards laughed uproariously as Jacob struggled to his feet and limped behind us on our way to work. Being a disgraced kapo in front of the other prisoners meant his job had ended, and he would probably go with the next contingent to the gas chamber. In spite of it, he played his role throughout the day as well as he could, perhaps thinking he might become an exception to the rule.

We started our painting task in the sleeping rooms that were assigned to one or more officers according to rank. From experience, I knew many of them kept boxes of pistol bullets in their footlockers, and during the week I managed to swipe twenty shells, tucking two at a time into both toes of my shoes. I also got some matches. It was easy to pull off, thanks to a dull-witted guard who didn't search our shoes at the after work inspections.

I had material for a bomb.

"Someone is planning to make a bomb and blow up the main gate," I whispered to Lieutenant Gruber. "That's the rumor I heard."

His eyes lit up in delight.

"Excellent work, Cain. Tell me everything."

"I don't have the details yet, Lieutenant, but I will in a few days. It's important you don't allow any inspections of the barracks until I report back to you. I want to get all the names and plans and find out where the material is stashed."

"All that isn't necessary. We can just shoot everybody from your barracks at roll call. That would be the efficient way to handle it."

"The thing is, when I give you the whole spiel, you'll be able to arrest the perpetrators, present them and the evidence to Colonel Deutscher and get a letter of commendation and probably a promotion."

He pondered this a moment, studying me with narrowed eyes.

"All right, Cain. I'll give you three days to get it together. If you're not playing straight with me, you'll get thrown into one of the ovens alive."

"Don't worry."

The next morning, using pliers smuggled out of the tool room by Myron the repairman, I emptied powder from the bullets into a casement made from a carafe that David, a sondercommando, had pilfered from the storeroom where confiscated belongings of new arrivals were kept. I packed it with slag metal, also supplied by Myron, fashioned a fuse from strands of cotton clothing, moistened it with lamp oil and *voila!* we had a bomb. Carefully, we pried some floorboards loose, and stashed it below. That evening, we were going to explode it under the north guard tower and make a run for freedom through the shattered barbed wire.

Before dark, we picked straws to see who would dash across the space to the tower and light the bomb. The job fell to me and I saw expressions of relief on the surrounding faces. I'd played the "long straw" trick, placing the unwanted long one higher than the others so that no one would choose it; I didn't want to mystify anyone with a show of self sacrifice. Prisoners in the other barracks had been alerted about the break, our new kapo Bernhard was in on it, and barring an informer, havoc was about to break loose.

I had just twenty seconds before the searchlight

came around, to run to the tower, light the fuse, and sprint out of range of the blast. Slowly, I opened the barracks door and peeked out. No obstructions, it was a go. I scanned the faces around me before I went, and their eyes were limpid, brave and alert. They looked truly human for the first time. "Go with God," someone whispered.

Running. I had never felt such clarity and power, as though moving with a whirlwind, a swirling galaxy, God himself. The camp didn't exist, nor my limited self, just primal force.

Running.

I was brought back to the moment by the sound of shouts: "Shoot him! Shoot him!"

I reached the base of the tower, set down the bomb, lit the fuse and sprinted away.

It exploded with a mighty force, toppling the tower, blasting open the barbed wire.

There was a collective yell of joy as prisoners from all over the camp swarmed out of their barracks in a tidal wave and rushed across the grounds, toward the blown fence.

The machine guns began chattering, men women and children fell, others ran through the hole and the machine guns sought them and riddled them with bullets. Some of the fallen called out "adonai." Soldiers gave chase and brought more of us down with rifle fire.

We ran.

The earth began to tremble from the roar of an approaching armada of a thousand British and American bomber planes overhead, silhouetted in the bright moonlight.

The soldiers stopped and looked at the sky.

We ran.

~.~

8

EVENINGS IN EDEN, we took our meals sitting crosslegged before the enchanted garden, contemplating its glow behind the flaming sword. The cherubim who guarded it cavorted happily and seemed to welcome our presence, though we knew they would never let us enter.

Adam and Eve would sometimes reminisce about the time before the Fall, when they lived in innocent bliss. The ending seemed strange to me.

"That wasn't fair!" I blurted out once, after the banishment segment. "You didn't know any better."

"Hush Cain," said father. "We did know better. We were given the rules and we broke them."

"But why did God make the serpent so deceptive and tricky he could outsmart you and mother?" asked Abel. "Was that right? Why didn't he show mercy?"

Dr. Eloi remained silent throughout this session, not interrupting to guide the flow or raise any questions. I was barely aware of him.

"You're asking questions we can't answer," said mother. "All we know is what happened. We failed when we were tested, and now we live like this, outside the garden. God is powerful and mysterious in his ways, and we have to accept that."

"Sometimes I wonder if it wasn't all done on purpose so that you would have to fail, and learn about good and evil," I said.

Father lost patience with me at this point and told me to fear God and hold my tongue.

"But I don't want to fear God! I don't want to fear anything!"

Glowering angrily, Adam slapped me across the face and I fled to the grain field, sulked and wept. Abel came to join me in a while. He had been crying too. Whenever father punished me Abel suffered empathetically, as though he were a silent partner in my transgression. Tender and obedient, Abel had been cast as the good boy, and I the not-so-good. I confess a part of me resented him from the day he was born, when he became the new source of my parents' joy. This wasn't any classic textbook case of "sibling rivalry," because I also loved him and delighted in his company. The part of me that simmered in envy was in abeyance but subtly coiled around my heart the way the serpent was coiled around the Tree of Knowledge.

"Stop crying brother," I said. "Let's do something. Let's have a race."

"All right."

Whooping in joy, we ran across the field, doubled back and ran it again several times until we were exhausted and fell onto the ground. We did some ribtickling wrestling, laughed aloud, and lay on our backs watching cherubic clouds breeze across the sky.

At moments like this I understood what life must have been like in the garden.

"Do you think we carry Paradise in our hearts?" asked Abel.

"I don't know. Maybe that's why we know happiness sometimes."

As if to demonstrate the opposite, a scorpion sauntered lethally toward Abel, its tail poised in sting position. I grabbed a stone, crushed it and threw its remains to a crow noisily squawking nearby. The crow hopped away to devour its meal, a jackal dashed from behind a pile of rocks, killed the crow and ate it. Before nightfall, a lion would kill the jackal, and the following day Adam would kill the lion with a spear ere it attacked a lamb that strayed from Abel's flock.

Kill, eat. What a strange business, that we creatures were made to take our nourishment from the slaughter of others.

Mother said nothing ever died in the garden, but

was transformed into other forms, a sprig to a bush, a weed to a rose, moss to grass, a spring to a creek, a hare to a gazelle, in a charmed cycle that never repeated itself and never ended. She said God would appear in the garden at times, in physical form, to spend time with her and Adam, and was always kind and never stern. When she invoked that time, her careworn features would soften and radiate a serene joy, her eyes a sad nostalgia. Adam, too, was transformed when he spoke of the garden. Our patriarch with the lined, weathered face became a grinning young man for the while, spirited, humorous, and oddly innocent.

We learned not to prod them about the garden overmuch, lest the memory become worn and less precious.

Abel's job was to shepherd the flock, and I tilled the soil. Adam oversaw our tasks and helped us, limping about on a withered leg that had been damaged in a mountain tumble.

There was always work to do, along with the flock and the fields. Water had to be drawn and carried from the river, our shelter repaired, clothes and blankets fabricated from the skins of animals and strands of plants, meat and vegetables put out to dry in the sun, tools and weapons made, vessels and furniture fashioned from fallen trees, stones set in the ground to form our paths.

And we had weather.

Unlike the sweet temperate climate of the garden, we had harsh weather that came with a vengeance—torrential downpours, floods, searing heat, droughts that left the parched, bloated bodies of dead animals lying about, icy winds, spirit-numbing fog. There was the volcano that terrified us, spewing magma and hot ashes dangerously close to our abode, and there was the awesome shaking and cracking of the land when earthquakes rumbled.

Our days proceeded in the paradigm of yang and yin, periods of difficulty relieved by spells of peace, overcast skies clearing to rays of sunshine.

The Lord our parents had spoken of so many times visited my brother and me one morning as we walked along the river bank. He wasn't in human form but manifested as brilliant light emanating from a balsam tree. ***"Cain. Abel."*** We stopped to listen. The voice was resonant and mellow, a kind of celestial music in discourse. Despite our sudden awe and bewilderment, Abel ventured a reply:

"Yes, Lord."

"On the morrow each of you will bring me an offering of the fruits of your labor."

There were no words beyond that. The tree bathed us in cordial effulgence for perhaps an hour, warming our marrow, and when it faded we fell asleep. On waking, Abel said he had dreamed scenes of such cosmic splendor that he hadn't words adequate to describe them, a panorama of universal beauty, galaxies in myriad colors moving raptly to the rhythm of time. Conversely, I'd had disturbing dreams of struggles with monsters, rejection by loved ones, exile, self-loathing, bizarre adventures without resolution. The dreams had put me in a dark mood, and I was envious that Abel had been graced with such finer drama.

The next morning before sunrise, we set our offerings in a clearing for God to see. I'd winnowed a bowl of the finest kernels of grain from my field and Abel had slaughtered the firstborn and most beloved of his flock, that he placed on a cloth, tears flowing from his eyes. He had never killed one of his sheep before, and it was hard for him. Before that, Adam had done the slaughtering, to spare Abel the horror.

Immediately I understood the truth I had suppressed all these years: Abel's offering was truly the better. He had sacrificed part of himself, along with the animal.

I sensed Dr. Eloi was aware of my insight, though he remained silent. We communed quietly for a while in contemplation, like climbers who had reached the peak of a high mountain. I told the rest of the story matter of factly, relieved of a certain tension.

The benign effulgence of God we had witnessed at the riverbank settled on Abel's offering, the animal returned to life and staggered off. The bowl of grain I had offered was shrouded in darkness. There was no acceptance, no acknowledgment. I looked at Abel kneeling before the cloth, his arms raised to the sky reverently, and I became furious. I couldn't comprehend why my offering wasn't elevated the same as his. What more could I do? It hurt more than I could stand; my thoughts were obscured by anger, I wanted to kill.

Abel, smiling dreamily, walked off behind the revived sheep to join his flock. I glanced at the pathetic bowl of grain shadowed in dreary obscurity, my heart ablaze in rage, picked up a branch, followed my brother, struck him on the head and watched him fall. I struck him again as he lay there, pulled his dead body into a ditch, covered it with dirt and leaves, and ran. I ran until I could run no more and collapsed exhausted to the ground.

The voice came again, this time stern and harsh:

Where is your brother Abel?

I answered defiantly:

"I don't know. Am I my brother's keeper?"

The voice of your brother's blood cries out to me from the ground.

The rest is the tale told perpetually-- the curse, the mark, condemnation to wander the earth ceaselessly.

Of God's admonishments, one recurs to me most often:

What have you done?

~.~

9

DR. ELOI informed me there would be an interval in our meetings because he had to tend to important matters elsewhere. He recommended that before we meet again, I explore the dilemma of the father.

The significance of this was unclear, and I was left to reflect on an intricate entanglement of God, Adam, social prohibitions, and the badgering of my own conscience.

~.~

10

THIS IS THE TRUE testimony and will of Adamo Gennesseo, father of Conti and Aberto Gennesseo, twins born to Eva Constanti, grand diva of the Opera Milano, on April 10, 1861.

To each of the aforementioned sons I leave a fourth of what I own, and to my legally married wife Francesca I leave the remaining half. All my properties and possessions are to be liquidated, and the revenue dispersed to those heirs exclusively.

"What are you doing?" Francesca called from the drawing room.

"Nothing, some calculations." I slid the paper between pages of Plutarch's Lives, where she would never venture, and returned the tome to the bookcase.

She entered the library.

"Are you ready? We mustn't be late."

She glanced at some crumpled papers in the wastebasket, making a mental note, perhaps, to peruse them later.

"Let's go, then."

"La Scala," I commanded Guiseppe, as we got into the coach.

"The opera, sir"

"Yes, Rigoletto tonight. I've arranged for you to sit backstage with the stage crew again but you mustn't pinch the chorus girls. The Maestro told me they complained about you last time."

"I'm innocent, sir."

"Nonetheless. Watch your hands."

"Yes sir."

Francesca laughed. "Naughty old man."

Guiseppe shrugged and snapped the reins.

As usual on an opening night, the opera house was packed. The front orchestra section where we sat was interspersed with the lights of society and smelled of perfume and a clothy aroma of wool, cotton and silk.

The house darkened, chatter faded, the orchestra struck up the overture and the brutal melodrama began.

Eva played the hunchbacked jester's doomed daughter Gilda, looking believably like an ingenue, thanks to skillful makeup and a still lissome figure. I saw that Francesca's dark eyes were burning as she followed the tragedy of the murdered daughter and the duped father. She was much more an opera lover than I, and one of the first to spring to her feet in wild applause after Gilda's heart-rending "Caro nome". Tears streaked her face at the finale when Rigoletto held the daughter whose death he had unwittingly abetted.

"Shall we visit?" I asked.

"Of course!"

We stood amidst baskets of flowers that spilled outside her dressing room.

A male voice answered the knock. "Yes! Who is it?"

"Adamo. And Francesca."

"Let them in!" Eva exclaimed.

Rigoletto opened the door, no longer a hunchback, stooped, or wearing a grey-streaked wig, but surprisingly youthful. Eva introduced us, he kissed her forehead and left the room.

"Well, cousin? How was I?"

"Superb!" said Francesca

"You were never better," I said.

After we chatted a few minutes, the theater director flung open the door and led a distinguished-looking man into the room, the king himself, Victor Emmanuel. He acknowledged us with a bow, kissed Eva's hand and pled, "I wonder, if you would be so kind as to dine with me tonight."

It was the first time I had seen her abashed.

"Why, why, yes...I would be honored," she said.

"Excellent. Then I will have my coachman come for you in an hour, if that's convenient. Til then."

There'd be no opportunity to discuss some delicate matters with Eva, so I surreptitiously placed on her dresser a letter I'd written, and we said our goodbyes.

The letter said that on my last visit to the orphanage, the boys complained she hadn't visited for a long while, and they missed her. It also said I was despondent about the charade, and wanted to confess the whole story to Francesca, who I felt was strong enough to understand and forgive. After all, Francesca hadn't been my wife when the pregnancy occurred, though we'd been courting.

I suggested it would be good for the boys if we visited them together soon, took them to dine, gave them some sort of family sense. I asked that a reply be carried between our manservants, arranging a time. Her answer was that she was terribly busy at present, but liked the idea and would look for a gap in her hectic schedule. Apparently, the king's attentions would be occupying her leisure, for a while.

Aberto and Conti were fraternal, not identical twins, and resembled each other but not closely. Conti was larger, golden-eyed like Eva and had curly hair like myself. Aberto's hair was straight, his eyes dark brown. He tended to be a dreamer whereas Conti was of the moment. Despite their differences, they had a strong rapport and enjoyment of one another and were safe from harassment from any of the other privileged orphans, because anybody who bedeviled one had to deal with both. I was very fond of them and dreamed of getting them out of the orphanage and raising them as my own. Keeping the secret from Francesca had become maddening, and it was time to end it.

My fantasy was, after she met the boys and got over the hurt, she would be charmed by them and become a skillful and loving stepmother. After all, she shared common blood with them, and too, mothering might ease the grief she'd endured ever since doctors had told her a uterus malformation rendered her incapable of childbirth.

When they were quite young, I told Conti and Aberto the truth about the events of their birth and they accepted it, in the way children accept truths that would be difficult for adults.

The parentage of children at "L'Ecole" was supposed to be a secret carefully guarded by the administration but secrets get out, and children taunted one another about their lineage, whether illustrious or middling.

The bastard son or daughter of a count or cardinal inspired more envy than the illegitimate progeny of a merchant, and could therefore fall prey to derision. Still, those with aristocratic blood felt themselves inherently superior to the others, and no amount of satire could diminish their implicit status. Our sons had no princely blood but could boast of artistic royalty through their renowned mother, with the lesser distinction of a father of vast wealth—chief exporter of Italy's olive oils and impresario of a thriving flower nursery, "Bounty of Eden."

"L'Ecole," so-named in French to evoke a luster of continental sophistication, was situated on the outskirts of the city on ten acres gracefully landscaped with lawns, hedges, flower beds, pathways, a variety of trees, a stream, a bridge. In keeping with the French motif, the residence building was scale-modeled after the Palace at Versailles and was divided into three sections, one housing boys, one for girls, and a third for infants and tots. In most cases, upon reaching age eighteen, the "graduates" were placed in a university or the military, if boys, or a suitable position, hopefully marriage, if girls. Efforts to allay peccadillos between adolescents and keep the girls at L'Ecole purely virginal did not always succeed, and occasionally, bastardization repeated itself unto another generation.

Dr. Eloi, the institute's director, was enthusiastic about contests, as were most of the parents (those who bothered to visit), the other faculty members and the children themselves. He staged spelling contests, tugs of war, pony races, cooking contests, costume competitions and road races on fancy English bicycles. There was always some contest looming to charge the atmosphere and keep spirits up.

Eva had persuaded the king to judge the latest, a boxing contest between some of the boys, to be guided safely by the new Marquess of Queensbury rules, and equipped with well-padded gloves.

At age 13, Aberto and Conti were physically and mentally vigorous, with a good deal of self-confidence. I was sure they'd fare well in the matches and bring honor to the bloodline of Gennesseo.

It was an early Fall afternoon, an idyllic day at L'Ecole, flowers blooming, insects flitting about, birds chirruping, a sweet aroma of plant and soil. The charm of nature belied the aggressive contests that were to begin on a platform on the lawn.

The parents, along with faculty, some visiting educators from America, and the king and his entourage, were ensconced on a stand built for the occasion that was festooned with garlands of flowers entwined around four supporting beams and shaded by a canopy of purple silk. Victor Emmanuel, flanked by Eva and two guard captains, was seated in the front row along with Dr. Eloi and the school's physician. At the conclusion of the matches the king was to present a silver medallion to the fighter he adjudged to be outstanding champion of the day.

Before the fray began, Eva and I visited Aberto and Conti in the spacious suite they occupied. As always, I was delighted to see them. Of course, they were most excited by the appearance of Eva, who hadn't been there for two months.

"When can we come to hear you in the opera?" asked Aberto.

"You promised," said Conti.

"And truly, I will keep my promise," she said. "I will have you brought to the last performance of Rigoletto and afterwards, at my house, my cook will make the finest meal you ever had."

"Do you promise on Heaven?" asked Conti.

"I promise on Heaven and Earth."

There was always a sad undertone to our visits, the shared and vulnerable awareness of abandonment that was the plight of all L'Ecole children, and parents had to deal with a sense of betraying their offspring, casting them as pariahs for the sake of expediency. Early on, when they learned to speak, the boys would ask when they were coming home and it pained me to have to repeat that this was their home, their mother and I had separate lives, my lawful wife didn't know of their existence, this was the best that could be done.

They accepted the inevitable, as children will, and the queries about "home" tapered off and ceased.

They did have a good life at the institute. Any staff member who proved to be less than loving and competent was discharged and replaced by someone more satisfactory. Dr. Eloi had a clear eye for discerning the abilities of his teachers, coaches, housemothers, maids. Even gardeners, repairmen, accountants were selected on the basis of their knack at relating to the children in a humane and instructive way.

After all, his clients were the elite of society, ranging from the newly rich to the grandees of aristocracy.

I did some mock boxing with the boys, enjoined them to do their best. Eva and I kissed and embraced them and returned to the spectators stand.

The contenders were approximately matched by age and weight so that our thirteen-year-olds came on midway through. Aberto was pitted against a somewhat larger, more aggressive boy who would have been more aptly matched with Conti. In the first round Aberto fared badly, getting hit often, his nose bloodied, knocked down once. In the second and third rounds he mustered confidence, outmaneuvered his opponent, kept him off balance, landed forceful punches on his face, chest and midriff. The athletic coaches declared Aberto winner and he was cheered enthusiastically, obviously a popular fellow.

Conti's match was the briefest of the day, a rout. In the first minute, he rained so many blows on his adversary that the referee stopped the fight, declaring it a mismatch. The applause for this was perfunctory as the loser walked off weeping in pain and humiliation. I had observed a cruel streak in Conti during the match, that surprised me. Ordinarily, he displayed a sunny, friendly disposition and I was vaguely troubled by this glimpse at his dark side.

The day's sport ended with a bout between two seventeen-year-olds who were clearly halfhearted about engaging in fisticuffs. They circled, feinted, landed some light to medium punches, danced a charade of aggression until it ended and one was marginally declared a winner.

Girls from the dance class performed a ballet for the king while he pondered who would receive the medallion for outstanding participant. The music maestro and his wife provided orchestration, he on violin, she on flute, until a wee girl costumed as a sprite skipped among the spectators sprinkling flower petals.

The king rose.

"I bestow the award of the medallion on Aberto Gennesseo who in my estimation showed great valor in overcoming difficulty and prevailing over a strong opponent. It is my wish that this champion shall someday become an officer in my honor guard."

Applause.

Aberto came forward and kneeled like one of the knights he had seen pictured in a book on chivalry. As the king placed the ruby-studded amulet around the boy's neck, the sun emerged from a cloud and heightened the drama, glinting sharply on the metal so that onlookers had to squint.

I was disturbed to see that Conti, glowering, broke away from the proceedings and ran off, into a grove of trees.

I assumed he would get over it. The day had peaked. Eva and I said our goodbyes to Aberto, congratulated Dr. Eloi, and left, she in the king's carriage, me driven by Guiseppe.

The old man interrupted my musing on how I would explain the day's absence to Francesca—a fib about overseeing a shipment of oil to America. I was unhappy with the lie and with lying.

"The boys were outstanding, sir, a fine pair of scrappers. You must be proud of them."

"Yes, they're good boys, Guiseppe."

Recalling Conti's flight, I mulled over his rage and regretted Eva and I hadn't been able to say goodbye to him. I wondered if envy of his brother was behind Conti's resentful snit, and tried to envision whether I had unknowingly showed favoritism to Aberto over the years—but no, I loved them equally. What was it, then?

That night I told Francesca everything. She was at first stunned into silence, staring at me with wide eyes, then became livid, screaming:

"You deceived me! All these years a secret family with my own cousin! You've been laughing at me! I've been so stupid! I hate you! I hate you!"

She threw some precious glassware at the wall, flung a paperweight into a mirror and proceeded slapping me on the chest and face. I didn't resist. She let out one more piercing scream and ran up the stairs.

"Francesca, please," I pleaded.

"Shut up," she shrieked. "Don't come near me."

She came down the staircase in a short while, carrying a satchel of clothing. Her personal maid Teresa was with her.

"Francesca, please."

"Don't talk to me you pig. I'm leaving. I'll send for the rest of my things."

She slammed the door and was gone.

I called to her through an open window: "Francesca, don't go! I love you! I love you!"

She reacted as I knew and feared she would, and she was absolutely right. At least she was authentic; I never could stand martyrs. With luck, perhaps, I could win her back. What horror, and it was all my own doing. When Teresa came for Francesca's possessions, I'd send a note offering to trade places, that is, move myself into a suite and let her come back to the estate.

I slept wretchedly that night, in sporadic clumps. During a fitful doze I dreamed the Devil was subsuming me, leering, extracting my soul, and I reached for the comfort of Francesca, touching only her absence.

The darkness was surreal, holding a terror I'd never known before.

In the morning I hastened to the front door on hearing a gentle knocking. I prayed it was Francesca, come back to me. But no, it was the Literature teacher from L'Ecole, looking pale and distraught. He had trouble meeting my eyes.

"Yes?"

"There's been a terrible incident at the orphanage."

I felt suddenly dizzy and groundless.

"What happened?"

"Aberto is dead, killed by his brother."

"No! What are you saying?" I grabbed him by the shoulders and shook him. "What are you saying?"

"It's true, signore Gennesseo, I'm sorry, it's true."

I let go of him and he staggered against the wall and broke into tears.

"Stop that crying. Tell me what happened."

"Nobody knows why, but for some reason, Conti, in a fury, ran up to Aberto in the courtyard and hit him with all his might. Aberto fell against the corner of a stone table and his skull was broken. This was witnessed by the gardener and one of the maids. Conti then tried to revive his brother until he saw it was impossible, and fell on Aberto's body, repeating, "What have I done, what have I done?" Then he stood, raised his eyes to the sky and yelled, "I hate you!" He ran off toward the river and into the forest. We searched all night and couldn't find him."

I was too stricken to do anything but collapse onto the sofa in a daze.

"You may go," I muttered.

"I'm so sorry, signore, so sorry."

I sat staring vacantly for perhaps two hours. The housekeeper, Maria, who had overheard, entered the salon intermittently to place her hands on my shoulders, dry my tear-streaked face, murmur softly.

"Maria," I finally managed to say.

"Yes, sir."

"He's dead."

"Yes."

"I wish it was me, not him."

"I understand."

"I don't know what to do."

I pictured Conti fleeing, aghast at himself, and I had a powerful fear I'd lose him too, the last thread of my family gone forever.

I knew what anguish he must have been in and I knew what I must do: find him and bring him home.

I called for Guiseppe to mount the carriage, and get us to L'Ecole as fast as the horses could move.

Eva was there when we arrived, sitting by Aberto's coffined body in the chapel. The priest was reciting a liturgy as brilliant sunlight poured through the stained glass windows, evoking a contradictory ambience of peace and beauty. I sat beside her, reached for her hand and we communed in a numb, bewildered silence. Aberto's face was pale and mottled, though his expression was serene, conveying his native gentleness.

I asked the priest if a departed spirit could forgive his killer and thereby release his sin. He replied only God could do that, but that wasn't what I wanted to hear.

"What if the killer didn't mean to kill?"

"It's in the hands of God, that's all I can tell you."

I felt oppressed by this God. Who was he? Was his nature as harsh, judgmental, whimsical, vain, punitive as humans supposed, or had they ascribed their own abysmal pettiness to him? I wondered if he even existed, beyond a mortal need for explanations.

A procession of orphans filed through the chapel, each setting a rose on Aberto's casket, crossing themselves, bowing to Eva and me.

"I'm going to find Conti," I whispered to Eva, and left.

As I stepped outside a brightly colored snake slithered out of the garden onto the stone path. I grabbed a hoe to kill it but it disappeared under some bushes, leaving me to wonder if I was seeing things, and why I had wanted to kill it in the first place.

The woods were shadowy when I got there, illumined by oblique rays of pale sunlight.

"Conti! Where are you? It's Adamo, your father. Please answer, my son. I know you're hurting. Please come. I want to take you home."

No answer. Occasionally the sound of some creature thrashing into the bushes gave me false hope. The woods got deeper, darker, gloomier, and the sound of my calling became muffled as though absorbed into the dank bark of the trees. Through the night I searched and called, and there was no response but the sound of branches moving in the wind. By dawn I found myself out of the woods in a stark landscape I had never known before. The ground was powdery grey, desiccated, sparsely strewn with jagged stones. Nothing moved, nor was there any sound. If Conti was there I would have known immediately, for there was nothing in view but desolation. It could have been purgatory or the moon.

"Conti! Where are you? Answer me."

I thought perhaps prayer might help, though it had never been a habit of mine. I sank to my knees.

"Lord, have mercy on my son who was wayward only in a fit of envy. I beg you. I'll do anything you ask of me. Have mercy on Conti who's only a boy."

The silence deepened as though that were the answer. I had no way to comprehend it.

Didn't this God mind that punishing one meant punishing many, or care that repercussions of condemnation spread through the world like a plague?

The sun rose cheerfully as though it were an ordinary day, and I walked on, eventually coming to a stream leading back to the forest. The forest was a relief in the morning's light, after the landscape of bleakness.

I continued to call for Conti and search the woods, to no avail. He could have gone to a nearby town, to the hills, to the seaport, there was no telling.

When I returned to the chapel Eva was alone, resting her head on the coffin, dozing. I sat beside her contemplating the remains of what had been our son.

She awoke and regarded me vaguely, as through gauze.

"Did you find him?"

"No."

"Where could he be?"

"I don't know. I'll search until I find him."

~.~

10

AND DID your father find you?

Not in Milan, perhaps in the expanse of his heart. I had fled to a place in Mexico where stories end.

I'm listening.

~.~

11

AT A CORRIDA in the Guanajuato mountains, I was last on the roster, one of four novice matadors appearing for the first time before a paying crowd.

The bulls in the three fights before mine had been dragged off after being killed sloppily and nervously by my predecessors. When I entered the bullring the crowd was poised skeptically, hoping, I supposed, for a more memorable performance than they had seen so far.

They would get it.

The ritualistic torment of the beast began with stabs from the lance-bearing picador, mounted on his padded horse. The aggressive young bull charged at the skittish horse straightaway, and the picador jabbed fearfully and too quickly at the creature's shoulders, so that strips of hide hung down exposing bloody flesh. There were boos of disgust when the picador finished and trotted to the exit, his eyes downcast, the horse swaying unsteadily. That fiasco was followed by the bandilleros sprinting to the side of the bull, plunging sharp pickets into the wounded area to heighten the pain and the flow of blood. The bull pursued them, bellowing in rage and agony, thrusting with its horns, until it was teased away by ring assistants who then scampered for safety. It snorted, leaped, circled about in confusion and pawed at the ground, not yet weakened by the profusion of blood streaming from its back. The patrons liked this animal. They stood, applauded, chanted "toro! toro! toro!."

When I entered the ring, the cheering diminished to an expectant silence as people craned forward to see if my performance would somehow redeem the art of bullfighting from the disgraces of the day. My obligation was to perform gracefully and bravely, let them relish triumph, witness the ritual done skillfully—tauntings with the cape, near brushes with goring or death, the ultimate flourish when the sword was plunged swiftly, adroitly, behind the animal's neck, piercing its heart.

"Ole! Ole!", they would shout, delighted at seeing mundane life transformed into myth.

I approached the bull. It didn't move, just watched me. The melodrama of the corrida faded into a vague backdrop as we gazed at each other for a timeless interval. In its eyes I saw a cyclorama of all murder since human life began. I saw the face of my brother as I last saw him when we played together on the grain field at

Eden. The knots in my heart unraveled and a torrent of relief rushed through my veins.

The spectators had risen to their feet and were watching silently, in rapt attention, as though trying to grasp something elusive.

I bowed to them, threw down the cape, threw down the sword, turned my back and walked away. The crowd roared thunderously. There was the sound of hoofbeats. There was the sweet fragrance of the Garden.

~.~

12

EVE REACHED for a portion of blue sky but it was too far away and she was dismayed to see her hand was empty. A fluffy little cloud covered the sun briefly, drifted away, and sunlight returned, radiating shimmering waves. She opened her palms to receive sunbeams and rubbed them gently onto Adam's back, interrupting his study of a bulge-eyed frog basking on a pink rock. He murmured "aaah," the frog croaked, and some dragonflies buzzed over to see what the commotion was. The sun rose higher and got warmer. Adam stood, took Eve's hand and they walked across the meadow to a pool encircled by roses, jasmine and gardenias, where a waterfall splashed onto their bodies and cooled them. When they got out, Adam immersed himself in a construction project, assembling twigs, leaves, stones, and mud into a fanciful structure. Eve was intrigued and helped, gathering bits of material, until she was distracted by a movement in the pomegranate tree. It was the serpent, coiled around a branch, looking down at them. She waved, and watched it in fascination for a while. It seemed to be a very wise creature. She wondered what she might learn from it.

~.~ ~.~